Gina and the Magic Bear

The Sound of Soft G

by Joanne Meier and Cecilia Minden • illustrated by Bob Ostrom

Published by The Child's World®
1980 Lookout Drive
Mankato, MN 56003-1705
800-599-READ
www.childsworld.com

The Child's World®: Mary Berendes, Publishing Director
The Design Lab: Design and page production

Library of Congress Cataloging-in-Publication Data
 Meier, Joanne D.
  Gina and the magic bear : the sound of soft G /
by Joanne Meier and Cecilia Minden ; illustrated by
Bob Ostrom.
    p. cm.
  ISBN 978-1-60253-402-5 (library bound : alk. paper)
  1. English language—Consonants—Juvenile literature.
2. English language—Phonetics—Juvenile literature 3.
Reading—Phonetic method—Juvenile literature. I. Minden,
Cecilia. II. Ostrom, Bob. III. Title.
  PE1159.M4565 2010
  [E]—dc22   2010002914

Printed in the United States of America in Mankato, MN.
July 2010
F11538

NOTE TO PARENTS AND EDUCATORS:

The Child's World® has created this series with the goal of exposing children to engaging stories and illustrations that assist in phonics development. The books in the series will help children learn the relationships between the letters of written language and the individual sounds of spoken language. This contact helps children learn to use these relationships to read and write words.

The books in this series follow a similar format. An introductory page, to be read by an adult, introduces the child to the phonics feature, or sound, that will be highlighted in the book. Read this page to the child, stressing the phonic feature. Help the student learn how to form the sound with her mouth. The story and engaging illustrations follow the introduction. At the end of the story, word lists categorize the feature words into their phonic elements.

Each book in this series has been carefully written to meet specific readability requirements. Close attention has been paid to elements such as word count, sentence length, and vocabulary. Readability formulas measure the ease with which the text can be read and understood. Each book in this series has been analyzed using the Spache readability formula.

Reading research suggests that systematic phonics instruction can greatly improve students' word recognition, spelling, and comprehension skills. This series assists in the teaching of phonics by providing students with important opportunities to apply their knowledge of phonics as they read words, sentences, and text.

The letter g makes two sounds.

The hard sound of **g** sounds like **g** as in: *go* and *gas.*

The soft sound of **g** sounds like **g** as in: *giraffe* and *huge.*

In this book, you will read words that have the soft **g** sound as in: *magic, orange, large,* and *giant.*

4

Gina likes to do magic tricks.

She uses a magic wand.

She likes to imagine things.

8

Gina has a bear named Gigi. Gigi is wearing a small, orange hat.

Gina waves her magic wand.

Gigi is now wearing a large red hat.

Gina waves her magic
wand again.

Gigi is now wearing orange shoes. They are too large for the bear!

Gina gives her bear a giant hug. Magic with you is such fun!

Imagine the magic you could do!

Fun Facts

Did you know that magic is divided into three categories? *Close-up magic* is magic that is performed with the magician standing close to audience members. This kind of magic may include tricks involving cards or coins. Magicians who do *parlor magic* usually perform farther away from the audience. Those who do *stage magic* typically perform on a stage in a theater.

Florida, California, Texas, and Arizona are the states that produce the most oranges. Orange trees were probably originally grown in Southeast Asia. When Christopher Columbus and other European explorers came to the Americas in the late 1400s and early 1500s, they brought orange seeds with them.

Activity

Preparing an All-Orange Lunch

If orange is your favorite color, invite your friends to a special lunch where everything you serve is the color orange. Foods you eat might include cantaloupe, orange Jell-O, yams, apricots, cheddar cheese, macaroni and cheese, toast with orange marmalade, or even actual orange slices! If you are thirsty, pour some orange juice or orange soda.

To Learn More

Books
About the Sound of Soft G
Moncure, Jane Belk. *My "g" Sound Box®*. Mankato, MN: The Child's World, 2009.

About Magic
Fox, Mem, and Tricia Tusa (illustrator). *The Magic Hat*. Orlando, FL: Harcourt, 2002.
Wyler, Rose, Gerald Ames, and Arthur Dorros (illustrator). *Magic Secrets*. New York: HarperCollins, 1990.
Yee, Wong Herbert. *Abracadabra! Magic with Mouse and Mole*. Boston: Houghton Mifflin, 2007.

About Orange
Cammuso, Frank, and Jay Lynch. *Otto's Orange Day*. New York: Little Lit Library, 2008.
Stewart, Melissa. *Why Are Animals Orange?* Berkeley Heights, NJ: Enslow Elementary, 2009.

Web Sites
Visit our home page for lots of links about the Sound of Soft G:

childsworld.com/links

Note to Parents, Teachers, and Librarians: We routinely check our Web links to make sure they're safe, active sites—so encourage your readers to check them out!

Soft G
Feature Words

Proper Names
Gigi
Gina

**Feature Words in
Initial Position**
giant

**Feature Words in the
Medial Position**
imagine
magic

**Feature Words in the
Final Position**
large
orange

About the Authors

Joanne Meier, PhD, has worked as an elementary school teacher, university professor, and researcher. She earned her BA in early childhood education from the University of South Carolina, and her MEd and PhD in education from the University of Virginia. She currently works as a literacy consultant for schools and private organizations. Joanne lives in Virginia with her husband Eric, daughters Kella and Erin, two cats, and a gerbil.

Cecilia Minden, PhD, is the former director of the Language and Literacy Program at the Harvard Graduate School of Education. She is now a reading consultant for school and library publications. She earned her PhD in reading education from the University of Virginia. Cecilia and her husband, Dave Cupp, live outside Chapel Hill, North Carolina. They enjoy sharing their love of reading with their grandchildren, Chelsea and Qadir.

About the Illustrator

Bob Ostrom has been illustrating children's books for nearly twenty years. A graduate of the New England School of Art & Design at Suffolk University, Bob has worked for such companies as Disney, Nickelodeon, and Cartoon Network. He lives in North Carolina with his wife Melissa and three children, Will, Charlie, and Mae.